Forgive Me?

Written and Illustrated by **Judy Link Cuddehe**

A **Found Link Book**   Herndon

For my beloved pack:

John, Mike, Johnny and Ding-Dong-Belle-the-Wonderdog

Found Link Books

Text and Illustrations Copyright © 2011 by Judy Link Cuddehe

Illustration mediums are acrylic, watercolor and digital.

ISBN 0-615-436013
ISBN-13: 9780615436012

I chewed your shoe.

I knew I should not,

as I gnawed,

tugged

and bit.

When a great big
hole appeared,

I poked my nose through it.

I made a mess.

I knew I should not,

but puddles are fun for me.

My muddy paws walked

everywhere!

I am to blame, sadly.

I ate your lunch.

I knew I should not,

but I did it anyway.

It tasted good,

but now I fear
that
you won't want
to play.

I barked and howled.
I knew I should not.

You were talking
on the phone.

I hope you will still
pat my head,

and feed me a
milk bone.

I broke your cookie jar.

I knew I should not,
    but I gave my tail a hard whirl.

Maybe

if I stare at you lovingly

you will still call me Good Girl.

I will try very hard
to be good and do right,
from early morning
until late at night.

Look into my eyes
and you will see
that I am as sorry as can be.

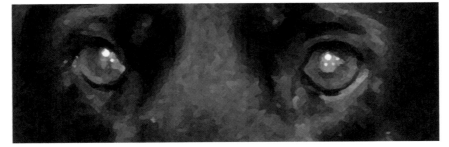

So, will you please

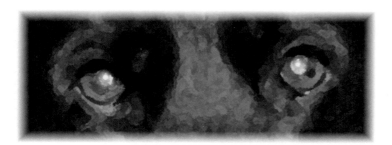

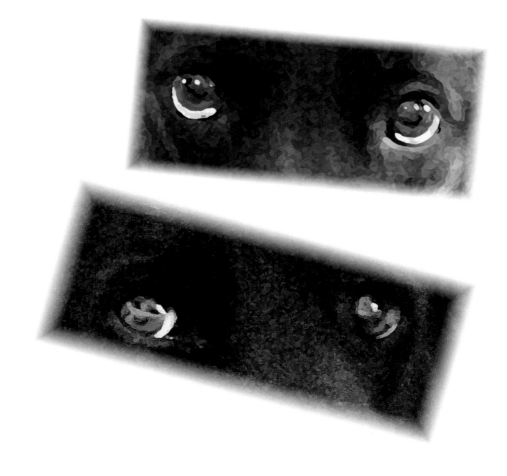

forgive me?

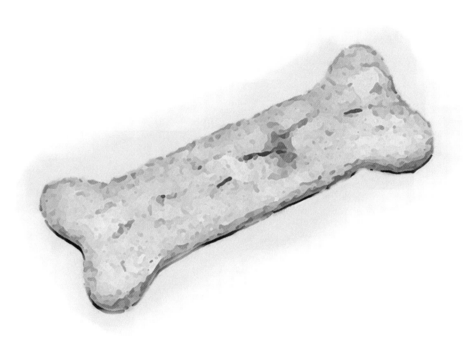

Found Link Books

An Animal Tale

CPSIA information can be obtained at www.ICGtesting.com
Printed in the USA
BVIW12n0245171216
471025BV00006B/26